W9-CBA-993

For Hannah,
all-by-herself
*M. W.*

For Georgie,
and Eddie Huntley
*P. B.*

Text copyright © 1992 by Martin Waddell
Illustrations copyright © 1992 by Patrick Benson

First U.S. edition 1992
Published in Great Britain in 1992
by Walker Books Ltd., London.
Library of Congress Cataloging-in-Publication Data
Waddell, Martin.
Owl babies / by Martin Waddell ; illustrated by
Patrick Benson.
Summary: Three owl babies whose mother has gone
out in the night try to stay calm while she is gone.
ISBN 1-56402-101-7
[1. Owls—Fiction.   2. Mother and child—Fiction.]
I. Benson, Patrick, ill.  II. Title.
PZ7.W1137Ow        1992
[E]—dc20              91-58750

20 19 18 17 16 15 14 13 12 11 10 9

Printed in Hong Kong

The pictures in this book were done with black ink and
watercolor crosshatching.

Candlewick Press
2067 Massachusetts Avenue
Cambridge, Massachusetts 02140

# OWL BABIES

Written by
## Martin Waddell

Illustrated by
## Patrick Benson

CANDLEWICK PRESS
CAMBRIDGE, MASSACHUSETTS

Once there were three baby owls:
Sarah and Percy and Bill.
They lived in a hole
in the trunk of a tree
with their Owl Mother.
The hole had twigs and
leaves and owl feathers in it.
It was their house.

One night they woke up and
their Owl Mother was GONE.
"Where's Mommy?" asked Sarah.
"Oh my goodness!" said Percy.
"I want my mommy!" said Bill.

The baby owls *thought*
(all owls think a lot) –
"I think she's gone hunting," said Sarah.
"To get us our food!" said Percy.
"I want my mommy!" said Bill.

But their Owl Mother didn't come.
The baby owls came out of
their house, and they sat
on the tree and waited.

A big branch for Sarah,
a small branch for Percy,
and an old piece of ivy for Bill.
"She'll be back," said Sarah.
"Back *soon*!" said Percy.
"I want my mommy!" said Bill.

It was dark in the woods and
they had to be brave, for things
*moved* all around them.
"She'll bring us mice and
things that are nice," said Sarah.
"I suppose so!" said Percy.
"I want my mommy!" said Bill.

They sat and they thought
(all owls think a lot) –
"I think we should *all*

sit on *my* branch," said Sarah.
And they did,
all three together.

"Suppose she got lost," said Sarah.

"Or a fox got her!" said Percy.

"I want my mommy!" said Bill.

And the baby owls closed
their owl eyes and wished their
Owl Mother would come.

AND SHE CAME.

Soft and silent, she swooped
through the trees
to Sarah and Percy
and Bill.

"Mommy!" they cried,
and they flapped and they danced,
and they bounced up and down
on their branch.

"WHAT'S ALL THE FUSS?"
their Owl Mother asked.
"You knew I'd come back."
The baby owls thought
(all owls think a lot) –
"I knew it," said Sarah.
"And I knew it!" said Percy.
"I love  my mommy!" said Bill.